W9-AZD-706

Larabee

story and pictures by

Kevin Luthardt

PEACHTREE
ATLANTA

Thank you Jesus, my Lord and Savior.

For my brother, Mike.

—*K. L.*

Published by
PEACHTREE PUBLISHERS, LTD.
1700 Chattahoochee Avenue
Atlanta, Georgia 30318-2112
www.peachtree-online.com

Text and Illustrations © 2004 by Kevin Luthardt

First trade paperback edition published in 2009

Paintings created in gouche, colored pencil, and acrylic on paper
Text typeset in Goudy Infant and titles in Handwriter

Book design by Kevin Luthardt
Book composition by Loraine M. Joyner and Melanie McMahon Ives

10 9 8 7 6 5 4 3 (hardcover)
10 9 8 7 6 (trade paperback)

Printed in June 2016 by RR Donnelley & Sons in China

Library of Congress Cataloging-in-Publication Data:

Luthardt, Kevin.
Larabee / written and illustrated by Kevin Luthardt.— 1st ed.
p. cm.
Summary: The mailman's dog, Larabee, helps deliver letters
and packages to everyone on the route except himself.

ISBN: 978-1-56145-300-9 (hardcover)
ISBN: 978-1-56145-482-2 (trade paperback)
[1. Letter carriers—Fiction. 2. Dogs—Fiction.] I. Title.
PZ7.L9793 La 2004
[E]—dc22
2003016994

This is Mr. Bowman. He is a mail carrier.
This is his dog. His name is Larabee.

RRRRRRR

RRIIING!!!

Every morning, Mr. Bowman
and Larabee wake up *very* early.

Larabee likes to ride in the mail truck.

He likes to help carry the mailbag too.

But most of all he likes the mail.
He wishes someone would send him a letter.

Larabee doesn't think that's fair.

Every day, Mr. Bowman and Larabee walk a long way. Sometimes they walk very slowly…

And sometimes very fast…

Little Benny Habermeyer
gets a birthday card.

Miss Calahan could have won
a million dollars.

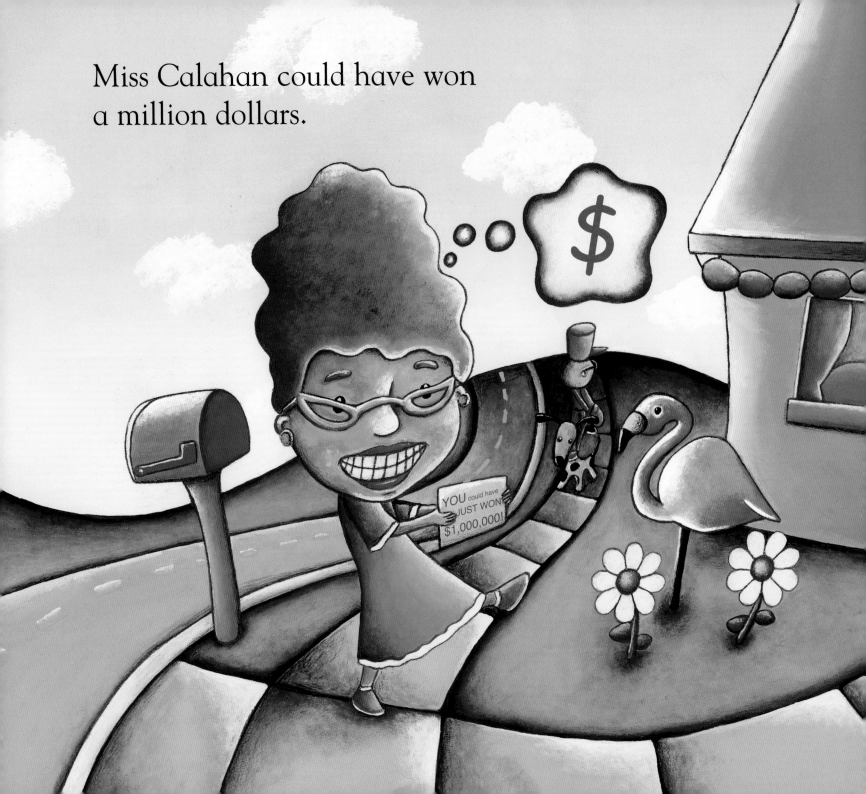

Mr. and Mrs. Mendoza get a letter from their son in the army.

Bruno the Butcher receives a large package.
What could be inside?

Larabee wishes he had a letter too…
But dogs don't get mail.

Everyone in town loves to see Larabee...

Except, of course, Mrs. Fellini.
She only likes cats.

But Lacey McNabb loves Larabee the most.

She gives him a great big hug
and ties flowers on his ears.

The mailbag
is empty.
All the mail
has been delivered.

But wait!
There's one
more letter!

It's for Larabee!

The End